One White Wishing Stone

A Beach Day Counting Book

Doris K. Gayzagian

illustrated by Kristina Swarner

NATIONAL GEOGRAPHIC
Washington, D. C.

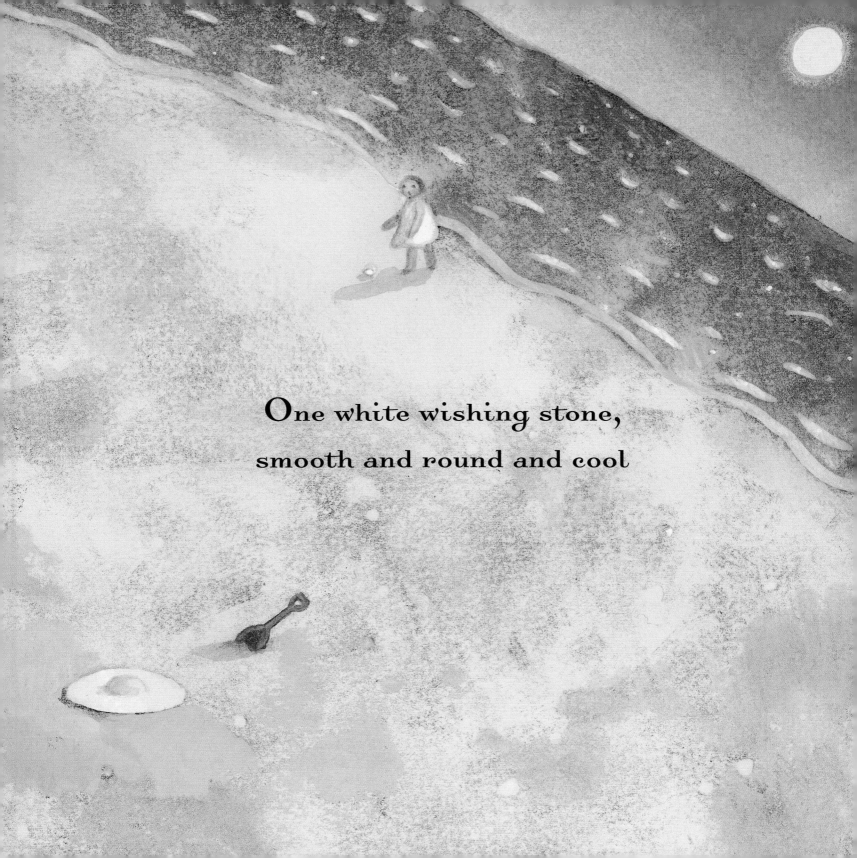

One white wishing stone,
smooth and round and cool

Two periwinkle shells

in a tidal pool

Three thistly cockleburs,
prickly and brown

Four soft seagull feathers

gently floating down

A five-fingered starfish scriggles in my hand.

Six strands of seaweed

straggle on the sand.

Seven striped scallop shells
slide inside my pail.

Eight skate egg cases—
each corner has a tail.

Nine bits of driftwood

sitting in the sun

Ten tiny sandpipers—
see how fast they run.

I make a castle in the sand
with walls and steps and towers
And trim it with the things I've found
and make believe for hours...

Until the tide comes whooshing in

with hungry tongues of foam

To eat my castle bite by bite

and take my treasures home.

But...

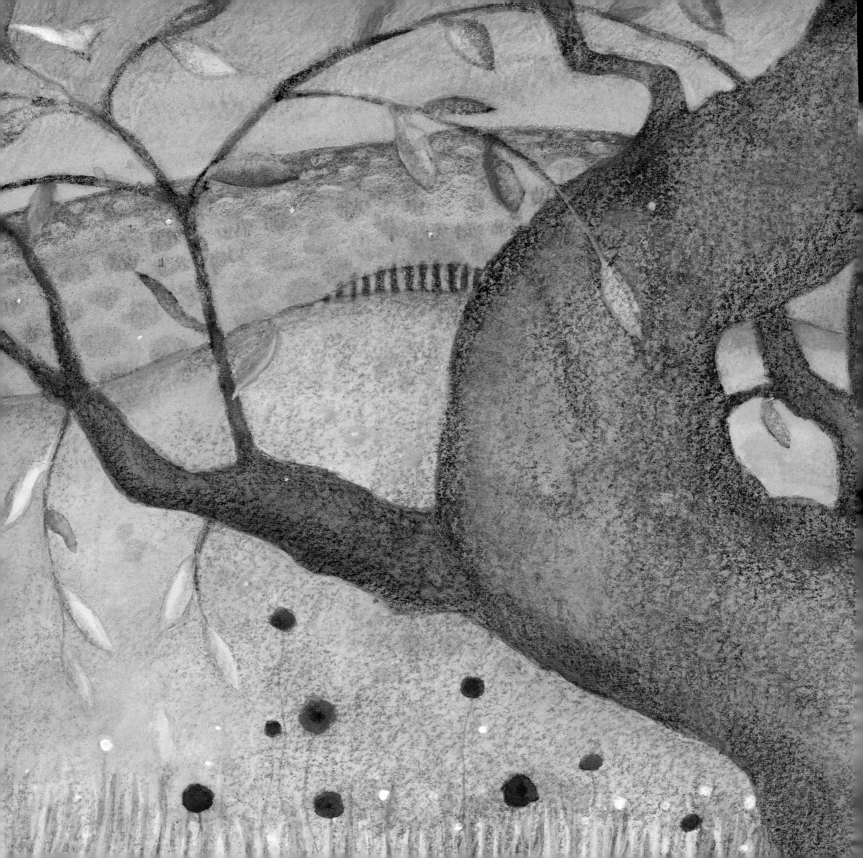

Two periwinkle shells
I save just for myself.
With one white wishing stone,
they'll sit up on my shelf.

When my mom comes in to get
a hug and goodnight kiss,
We'll wish upon the wishing stone
for another day like this.

Lovingly dedicated to my daughter
in memory of our many wonder-filled days
on Cape Cod Bay
—DKG

For John
—KS

Text copyright © 2006 Doris K. Gayzagian
Illustrations copyright © 2006 Kristina Swarner

Published by the National Geographic Society.

Illustrations are original prints colored using watercolor and pencil.
Book design by Bea Jackson
Text for this book is set in Dalliance Roman from Emigre, designed by Frank Heine.

For information about special discounts for bulk purchases, please contact
National Geographic Books Special Sales: ngspecsales@ngs.org

Library of Congress Cataloging-in-Publication Data is available from the Library of Congress upon request.
Trade ISBN-10: 0-7922-5110-5
Trade ISBN-13: 978-0-7922-5110-1
Library ISBN-10: 0-7922-5573-9
Library ISBN-13: 978-0-7922-5573-4

One of the world's largest nonprofit scientific and educational organizations, the National Geographic Society was founded in 1888 "for the increase
and diffusion of geographic knowledge." Fulfilling this mission, the Society educates and inspires millions every day through its magazines, books,
television programs, videos, maps and atlases, research grants, the National Geographic Bee, teacher workshops, and innovative classroom materials.
The Society is supported through membership dues, charitable gifts, and income from the sale of its educational products. This support is vital to
National Geographic's mission to increase global understanding and promote conservation of our planet through exploration, research, and education.

National Geographic Society
1145 17th Street N.W.   Washington, D.C. 20036-4688   U.S.A.
Visit the Society's Web site: www.nationalgeographic.com
Printed in the U.S.A.

DATE DUE
